Viking Thunder in Dublin

Oisín McGann

Illustrated by **Derry Dillon**

Published 2014
Poolbeg Press Ltd

123 Grange Hill, Baldoyle
Dublin 13, Ireland

Text © Poolbeg Press Ltd 2014

A catalogue record for this book is available from the British Library.

ISBN 978 1 78199 978 3

Cover design and illustrations by Derry Dillon
Printed by GPS Colour Graphics Ltd, Alexander Road, Belfast BT6 9HP

Viking Thunder in Dublin

This book belongs to

MAC – Mythical Activity Control

Mission Info

There was a time, long ago, when Ireland was a place of magic. Now, all the magical people and creatures live in the Otherworld. To people like you, they are just myths and legends. But sometimes they can escape into your world.

Mythical Activity Control guards the doorways to your world. And when someone gets through, it's MAC's job to bring them back.

From the Agent Files:

ÁINE *(pronounced 'AWN-yeh')*
Ancestor:
Aine, Goddess of
Summer and Light.
Personality:
Smart but stubborn.
Loves nature.
Can judge the moods of
people and animals.
Power:
Can talk to animals.
Can travel through
mirrors and polished metal.

FIONN *(pronounced 'Fy-UNN')*
Ancestor:
Legendary warrior Fionn McCool.
Personality:
Clever, sensible, but curious too
and that can get him into trouble.
Power:
Can connect to information from
either world by biting his thumb,
like his ancestor after he tasted
the Salmon of Knowledge.
Can travel through mirrors and polished metal.

TOGETHER, they help keep you safe from the
wild magic of the Otherworld.

Also in the MAC series

The Banshee Queen of Cork

On a dark and gloomy day, men were digging
holes in Dublin Zoo. They were building a new
space for the elephants. The engines of diggers
and dump trucks roared as the men worked.
Black storm clouds rumbled overhead.

Tom, the man in charge, checked his watch. It was late, nearly time to finish work for the day. Then Tom heard a cry and one of the digger drivers came running up. The man looked shocked and just a little bit scared.

"What's up, Joe?" Tom asked.

"We've found something!" Joe said. "It's . . . it's . . . You'd better come and see!"

Tom followed him to the deep hole that
Joe had been working on with his digger. He
gasped when he saw what Joe was pointing at.
Thunder boomed and lightning lit up the sky.

"Holy cow!" he cried. "What . . . what is it?"
Sticking up out of the hole was a large wooden
dragon's head. It was carved on a long, curving
neck. It had a long tongue, sharp fangs and
staring eyes.

"Everyone stop digging!" Tom shouted, waving his hands to the other workers there. "Stop digging! We're going to need some help here . . ."

Not far away, in O'Connell Street, the storm was getting worse. Right in the middle of the street, a tall steel sculpture reached up towards the clouds. It was the Spire of Dublin. It stood in the centre of the city like the mast of a ship.

Then a great finger of forked lightning shot down and struck the Spire.

A strange blue fire travelled down the metal and hit the ground near a tourist bus. A giant man rose up out of the fire and stepped out in front of the bus, making it skid to a stop. The people on the bus screamed as the wild-looking man hammered on the door . . .

Not long after the lightning struck the Spire, another strange thing happened. The shiny steel of the Spire shimmered and rippled and two children stepped out. Their names were Áine and Fionn. They were secret agents. They worked for MAC – Magical Activity Control.

It was their job to make sure no one from the Otherworld caused trouble in this world. And now someone was.

"This is where he came through," Áine said. She pointed at the burnt patch on the ground.

Fionn nodded and turned to look up at the Spire. The storm had died down, but the clouds were still dark.

"He came in on the lightning," he said. "Wish we could do that. It would be so cool to ride the lightning. But why did he come back? He hasn't been here in over a thousand years."

"It must be something important," Áine replied. "He knows he's not supposed to leave the Otherworld. Just wait till I find him! I'm going to –"

"What will you do?" Fionn interrupted her. He gave her a thump on the shoulder. "The guy's eight feet tall. He spent his whole life sailing rough seas and fighting battles. Let's not go picking any fights yet. How about we just find him first and see?"

"Okay," she sighed. "Let's ask around – find if anyone saw him."

She let out a whistle. The pigeons who were flying around the street heard her and flocked towards her, gathering at her feet. Fionn stepped back a bit. He didn't really like pigeons.

"Hi, you lot!" Áine said to the birds, talking to them as if they were people. "Can you give us a hand? We're looking for the big mean-looking guy who came down on the lightning. Did you see where he went?"

The pigeons all tried to answer at once, cooing and twitching their heads.

"One at a time! Please!" Áine cried, holding up her hands.

They went quiet and one of the pigeons warbled something at her.

"Really?" Áine said. "That's, eh . . . interesting."

She turned to look at Fionn. He wasn't like her. He couldn't talk to animals, so he had to wait to hear what the birds had told her. Áine frowned and pointed down the street towards the bridge that crossed the River Liffey.

"They said Olaf caught a bus," she told him.

"Yeah?" Fionn asked, raising his eyebrows. "I bet it's the first time a Viking has ever done that."

As agents of MAC, Áine and Fionn had to be able to move fast. They had the power to travel instantly through mirrors. They could jump in through a mirror in one place and out through a mirror somewhere else. The mirrors were magical doorways.

It was a lot faster than walking. Or taking the bus. Sometimes they could jump through polished steel like the Spire. But most of the time, they had to stick to proper mirrors. When you knew how to use them, mirrors could even carry you across to the Otherworld.

MAC controlled the mirror roads, so the roads obeyed Áine and Fionn's commands. They only had to think of the name of a place, or picture it in their minds and the roads could find the mirror that was nearest to it.

The two MAC agents tracked the bus that Olaf was riding. They jumped from one mirror to another along the way, appearing in one place after another. Áine spoke to a seagull with smelly breath on the River Liffey. Then she talked to a posh cat outside Trinity College. Then a friendly rat told them a mad Viking had just jumped off a bus outside Christ Church.

"Vikings used to attack churches, back in the old days," Áine said. "You don't think . . . ?"

They dived into a mirror in a clothes shop and came out through another into a hairdresser's. The women there screamed in shock. The two kids ignored them and ran out into the street.

"Christ Church is right where Olaf lived when he was King of Dublin," Fionn said, nibbling his thumb. "When Dublin was just starting off as a town. Let's see what's there now besides the church."

Fionn triggered his magical power by biting his thumb. When he did this, he could find information from the worldwide web in this world. Or he could search the myth-web in the Otherworld.

"Hurry up!" Áine said impatiently.

"Give me a second!" he snapped. Then his eyes opened wide and he took his thumb out of his mouth. "That Dublinia place is there! They've got loads of Viking stuff. Maybe that's where he's going!"

Two men were unloading a large mirror from a van outside the majestic Christ Church. The place looked a bit scary against the dark, gloomy sky. The men got the fright of their lives when two kids jumped out of the glass.

Fionn and Áine started running up towards the entrance to the Dublinia museum.

As they skidded to a stop in front of the doorway, they heard a voice shouting out: *"Stop him! Stop that thief!"*

Áine and Fionn looked up. The big door was smashed to pieces, as if someone had kicked it in. Fionn was about to say something when a huge man charged out. He was dressed in leather and fur. His arms were filled with helmets, axes, swords and shields.

He ran right through the children, sending them flying. Before they could pick themselves up, the Viking jumped on a packed tourist bus parked up the street. The driver was waiting, terrified of his new master. With a screech of tyres, he swung the bus away and they took off up the road.

"That was Olaf all right," Fionn muttered, rubbing his bruised head. "But what's he up to?"

"Don't know," Áine groaned. "But he just stole a load of Viking weapons and helmets from the museum. It looks like he's getting an army together. But for what?"

"And why now?" Fionn wondered. "Hang on a second . . ."

He bit his thumb and a few seconds later he gasped. He pressed his thumb against the window. It made the glass flicker like a television coming on. Then it showed Áine what Fionn could already see. It was a news report. It showed a crowd standing around a huge, deep hole in the middle of Dublin Zoo. Sitting in the hole was an old Viking ship.

"That's why he came back!" Áine groaned. "The zoo people found his old ship and now he wants it back!"

"Yeah. And he won't care who he has to hurt to get it!" Fionn said.

The two men carrying the big mirror yelped and shouted a warning as Áine and Fionn sprinted up and jumped straight at the shiny surface. The men stared in amazement as the two kids went right into the mirror and disappeared.

The two agents dived out of a mirror in one of the toilets in the zoo. Rolling up onto their feet, they ran outside. Olaf's old ship lay in its hole on the far side of the lake. It wasn't hard to find. There was a crowd around it, and lots of Guards standing protecting it. Áine and Fionn stopped when they saw the police.

Then the tourist bus crashed through the gates of the zoo. Olaf stood on the top at the front. He was roaring and waving an axe and shield. Black clouds rolled across the sky, thunder boomed and lightning flashed. The tourists on the bus had weapons, shields and helmets too, but they looked very scared.

"He's treating them like they're his crew on a ship," Fionn said.

"He'll try and break through the police," Áine said. "This could get ugly."

"He really wants that ship," Fionn sighed. "Maybe they should just give it to him?"

"They won't let him take it," Áine said. "But maybe . . . maybe we can keep them busy long enough to let him get to it . . ."

"It might stop people getting hurt," Fionn said. "Any ideas?"

"Just the one," she replied. "But it's a really good one."

The people ran for their lives as the Viking's bus charged across the zoo towards them. The Guards stayed where they were. The driver and his passengers howled in fright as the bus ploughed into a grassy bank. It shuddered to a halt in a flowerbed and Olaf leaped from the top, landing right in front of the police.

"I'm going aboard my ship!" he bellowed.

"You're going to jail!" one of the Guards shouted back.

"I'm going home!" the bus driver wailed, as he jumped off the bus and ran away.

It looked as if a huge fight was about to start, but then a strange sound carried across the zoo. The crowd fell silent and listened with fear. The sound was a cackling, grunting roar of wild voices. All the people looked round to see loads of animals running towards them. Elephants, giraffes, antelopes, buffalo and lots of other beasts swept around the crowd of people, galloping past.

Somebody had opened the gates and let them out. Just the fairly safe ones – not the lions or tigers. After all, Áine and Fionn didn't want anyone to get eaten.

All the zoo workers ran about, trying to round up all the animals. The Guards had to rush around trying to help. In all the madness, only Fionn and Áine saw Olaf climb into his ship. He spoke some old and magical words to it and it slowly lifted off the ground.

The storm was growing stronger. The ship rose up towards the sky. Olaf looked down at the two children and waved. Then he smiled. A bolt of lightning struck the ship and it disappeared in a flash of light.

"Lightning," Fionn said, shaking his head. "It really is the coolest way to travel."

"At least he's back where he belongs," Áine said. "Come on, we'd better go and help with these animals."

"Can't we look around first?" Fionn asked her. "I've never been to the zoo here."

Áine took a long look at the mess all around them.

"Why not?" she said. "Everyone else is pretty busy. At least we'll have a good view of the animals. I mean, the ones that are left."

And so, while the police and the zookeepers ran back and forth trying to catch the animals, Áine and Fionn hurried off to see the sights.

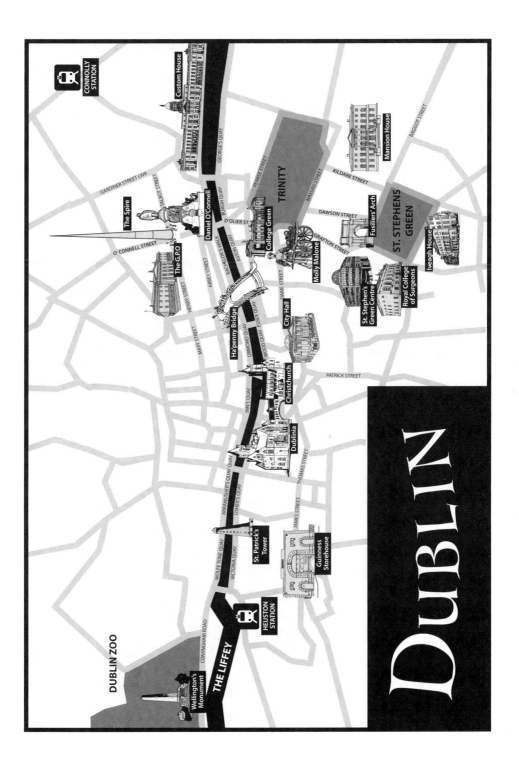

Ten Fun Facts About Dublin!

1. The word "Dublin" comes from the two Irish words "dubh" and "linn", meaning "black pool".

2. Dublin was founded by the Vikings.

3. Viking Dublin had the biggest slave market in Europe.

4. O'Connell Bridge was originally made of rope and could carry only one man and a donkey at a time.

5. The River Liffey swimming race has been run for nearly a hundred years, even back when the river was badly polluted.

6. The "Oscar" trophy, the world's most famous film award, was designed by a man from Dublin.

7. Jonathan Swift, the writer of *Gulliver's Travels*, was born in Dublin.

8. The song, "Molly Malone" is about a beautiful woman who sold fish. Nobody knows if she was ever real, but the song is so famous there is now a statue of her at the bottom of Grafton Street.

9. Dublin's most famous statues all have nicknames, like the "The Dolly with the Trolley" and "The Hags with the Bags". Some of the men's statues are called worse names.

10. Bram Stoker, the writer of *Dracula*, was from Dublin.

If you enjoyed this book from
Poolbeg why not visit our website:

www.poolbeg.com

and get another book delivered straight
to your home or to a friend's home.

All books despatched within 24 hours.

POOLBEG

Why not join our mailing list
at www.poolbeg.com and get some
fantastic offers, competitions,
author interviews and much more?

@PoolbegBooks